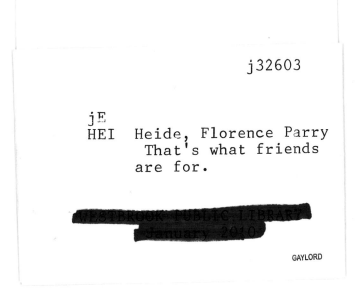

THIS CANDLEWICK BOOK BELONGS TO:

_____

_____

_____

To S. V. C., good friend then and now
F. P. H.

First Candlewick Press paperback edition 2007

The Library of Congress has cataloged the hardcover edition as follows:

Heide, Florence Parry.
That's what friends are for / Florence Parry Heide and Sylvia Van Clief ;
illustrated by Holly Meade. — 1st ed.
p.   cm.
Summary: All the elephant's friends give him advice, but none can solve his problem until
the opossum announces friends are to help, not just to give advice.
ISBN 978-0-7636-1397-6 (hardcover)
[1. Elephants — Fiction. 2. Animals — Fiction. 3. Friendship — Fiction.]
I. Van Clief, Sylvia. II. Meade, Holly, ill. III. Title.
PZ7.H36 Tg 2003
[E] — dc21   00-057207

ISBN 978-0-7636-2646-4 (paperback)

2 4 6 8 10 9 7 5 3 1

Printed in China

This book was typeset in Slimbach.
The illustrations were done in watercolor and cut paper collage.

Candlewick Press
2067 Massachusetts Avenue
Cambridge, Massachusetts 02140

visit us at www.candlewick.com

That's What Friends Are For

Florence Parry Heide and Sylvia Van Clief

illustrated by Holly Meade

CANDLEWICK PRESS

CAMBRIDGE, MASSACHUSETTS

Theodore the elephant
is sitting in the middle of the forest.
He has hurt his leg.

What a pity!
Today Theodore was going
to meet his cousin
at the end of the forest.

"What can I do?" Theodore says.
"My cousin is at the end of the forest,
and here I am in the middle of the forest.
And I have a bad leg, and I can't walk.

"I know what I'll do," Theodore says.
"I'll ask my friends for advice.
That's what friends are for."

Along comes Theodore's
friend the bird.

"Why are you sitting here
in the middle of the forest?"
asks the bird.

"Because I have a bad leg,
  and I can't walk.
  And I can't meet my cousin
  at the end of the forest," says Theodore.

"If *I* had a bad leg,
  I would fly to the end of the forest,"
  says the bird to Theodore.

"It's nice of you to give advice,"
  says Theodore to the bird.

"That's what friends are for,"
  says the bird.

Along comes Theodore's friend
the daddy longlegs.

"Why are you sitting here
in the middle of the forest?"
asks the daddy longlegs.

"Because I have a bad leg,
and I can't walk.
And I can't fly.
And I can't meet my cousin
at the end of the forest," says Theodore.

"If *I* had a bad leg,"
  says the daddy longlegs,
"I could walk anyhow—
  because I have seven other legs."

"It's nice of you to give advice,"
  says Theodore.

"That's what friends are for,"
  says the daddy longlegs.

Along comes Theodore's friend
the monkey.

"Why are you sitting here
in the middle of the forest?"
asks the monkey.

"Because I have a bad leg,
and I can't walk.
And I can't fly.
And I don't have seven other legs.
And I can't meet my cousin
at the end of the forest,"
says Theodore.

"If *I* had a bad leg," says the monkey,
"I would swing by my tail from the trees, like this."

"Well," says Theodore,
"I may have a very weak tail,
 but I have a very strong trunk."

Theodore grabs the
tree with his trunk . . .

Crash!

"Well, anyhow," says Theodore,
"thank you for your advice."

"That's what friends are for,"
says the monkey.

Along comes Theodore's friend the crab.

"Why are you lying down
in the middle of the forest?"
asks the crab.

"Because I have a bad leg,
and I can't walk.
And I can't fly.
And I don't have seven other legs.

"And I can't swing from the trees
by my tail (OR my trunk).
And I can't meet my cousin
at the end of the forest,"
says Theodore.

"If *I* had a bad leg," says the crab,
"I would get rid of it and grow another one."

"It's nice of you to give advice,"
 says Theodore.

"That's what friends are for,"
 says the crab.

Along comes Theodore's friend the lion.

"Why are you sitting here
in the middle of the forest?"
asks the lion.

"Because I have a bad leg,
and I can't walk.
And I can't fly.
And I don't have seven other legs.
And I can't swing from the trees
by my tail (OR my trunk).
And I can't grow another leg.
And I can't meet my cousin
at the end of the forest," says Theodore.

"If *I* had a bad leg," says the lion,
"I would roar so loud that
everyone would come running
to see what was the matter."

And he

roars.

"What's all the noise?"
 the opossum asks.
 He is hanging upside down by his tail.

"Theodore can't fly," says the bird.
"He can't get to the end of the forest
 to see his cousin," says the lion.
"We are giving him advice," says the crab.
"That's what friends are for."

"Nonsense," says the opossum.
"Friends are to *help*.
 Bring the cousin to Theodore."

So all the friends
go to find Theodore's cousin
at the end of the forest.

And they bring the cousin
to Theodore.

Theodore and his cousin
and all the friends are having a party.

"Thank you for *helping* me,"
says Theodore to his friends.

"That's what friends are for,"
say the friends.

To give advice is very nice,
but friends can do much more.
Friends should always help a friend.
That's what friends are for!

Florence Parry Heide is the award-winning author of more than fifty children's books, including the classic *The Shrinking of Treehorn*, illustrated by Edward Gorey, and *Some Things Are Scary*, illustrated by Jules Feiffer. She says, "One of my many (true) sayings is 'A new friend is around the corner of every single day.' Also true: Friendships last. And last." Florence Parry Heide lives in Wisconsin.

Sylvia Van Clief cowrote many books for young readers with Florence Parry Heide, including *It Never Is Dark*, *How Big Am I?*, and the Spotlight Club Mysteries. They also collaborated on *Songs to Sing About Things You Think About*, with Van Clief composing the music and Heide writing the words. Sylvia Van Clief died in 1974.

Holly Meade is the author and illustrator of *A Place to Sleep*, and has illustrated many acclaimed books for children, including *On Morning Wings* by Reeve Lindbergh and *Peek! A Thai Hide-and-Seek* and *Hush! A Thai Lullaby* by Minfong Ho, the latter of which is a Caldecott Honor Book. Of *That's What Friends Are For*, she says, "I just love the genuineness and warmth of this story. These well-meaning forest critters so completely miss the mark in helping their friend—thank goodness for the opossum!" Holly Meade lives in Maine.